# 淘氣一族

Terry Dinning 著

Angela Kincaid 繪

陳培真 譯

三民書局

Read with Me Stories ISBN 1 85854 749 0

Written by Terry Dinning and illustrated by Angela Kincaid

(Two stories: "Freddy Fox" and "Gilda the Witch")

First published in 1998

Under the title Read with Me Stories

by Brimax Books Limited

4/5 Studlands Park Ind. Estate,

Newmarket, Suffolk, CB8 7AU

My First Storybook ISBN 1 85854 517 X

Illustrated by Angela Kincaid

(One story: "The Naughty Kitten")

First published in 1996

Under the title Read by Yourself

By Brimax Books Limited

4/5 Studlands Park Ind. Estate,

Newmarket, Suffolk, CB8 7AU

# 巫婆姬達

## Gilda the Witch

It is morning in the forest. Gilda the witch **turns over** in bed. "Time for another little **snooze**," she says sleepily. Gilda takes care of the forest with her magic **spells**. Her cottage is full of magical things. She has a **broomstick**, a **cauldron**, a **crystal** ball and shelves full of books. She also has a cat called Timothy.

*turn over*
翻轉

*snooze* [snuz]
名 小睡

*spell* [spɛl]
名 咒語，魔力

*broomstick* [`brum,stɪk]
名 掃帚

*cauldron* [`kɔldrən]
名 大鍋

*crystal* [`krɪstḷ]
名 水晶

森林裡的早晨，巫婆姬達在床上翻了個身。「再小睡片刻吧！」她睏倦地說。姬達用她的魔法來照顧這片森林。她的小木屋裡滿是有魔力的東西。她有一把掃帚、一個大鍋、一顆水晶球、以及堆滿書的書架。她還有一隻名叫提摩西的貓咪。

**T**imothy leaps up onto Gilda's bed and **licks** the end of her nose.
"What is the matter Timothy?" **mumbles** Gilda. "Why are you waking me up?" She sits up in bed, and the tip of her witches' hat falls down over one eye. "What is that **noise**?" she **wonders**. She hears a strange noise outside.

*lick* [lɪk]
動 舔

*mumble* [ˋmʌmbl̩]
副 含糊不清地說

*noise* [nɔɪz]
名 嘈雜聲

*wonder* [ˋwʌndɚ]
動 納悶

提摩西跳到姬達的床上，舔了舔她的鼻尖。

「怎麼啦？提摩西？」姬達含糊地說。「為什麼你要叫醒我呢？」她在床上坐起身來，巫婆帽的末梢垂了下來，蓋住一隻眼睛。「那是什麼嘈雜聲啊？」她訝異地問，她聽到外頭有奇怪的聲音。

ilda leaps out of bed. Through the window she can see Katie and Bobby Rabbit scampering away in the **distance**. The sky is blue, the grass is green and the **daisies** are white and yellow. "How lovely!" **sighs** Gilda. "Today my spells will **sweeten** the bees' honey and make the roses smell like **perfume**."

*distance* [ˋdɪstəns]
名 遠處

*daisy* [ˋdezɪ]
名 雛菊

*sigh* [saɪ]
動 嘆息

*sweeten* [ˋswitn̩]
動 使變甜

*perfume* [ˋpɝfjum]
名 香水

姬達跳下床來。從窗戶望去，她看見小兔子凱蒂和巴比在遠處蹦蹦跳跳地跑開。藍色的天空，綠色的草地，還有黃白相間的小雛菊。

「多美麗啊！」姬達讚嘆著。「今天，我的魔法會使蜂蜜變得香甜，使玫瑰芬芳如香水。」

**G**ilda is **stirring** her cauldron when there is a **knock** at the door. It is Sally **Squirrel**. "Have you seen what has happened to the forest?" she **squeaks**.

Gilda hurries outside. The trees are as tall as ever. The flowers smell as sweet as ever. Then Gilda sees what is wrong. The sky is not blue. It is green! The grass is not green. It is blue!

*stir* [stɝ]
動 攪拌

*knock* [nɑk]
名 敲門聲

*squirrel* [`skwɝəl]
名 松鼠

*squeak* [skwik]
動 吱吱叫

姬達攪拌著她的大鍋爐，這時有人敲門。是小松鼠莎莉。「妳看到森林裡發生的事了嗎？」莎莉吱吱叫。
姬達衝到了外面。樹木和往常一樣高大，花兒和以前一樣地香，然後，姬達看見不對勁的地方了。天空不是藍色的，竟然是綠色的！草地不是綠色的，竟然是藍色的！

"One minute the sky was blue, and now it is green," says Sally. "You must **cast** a spell to make everything right again."

"I need my magic spell book," says Gilda. She **hunts** along the bookshelves. She hunts under the table. She hunts among the **cushions**. "Where did I put that spell book?"

*cast* [kæst]
動 施展

*hunt* [hʌnt]
動 尋找

*cushion* [ˋkuʃən]
名 墊子

「一分鐘以前天空還是藍色的，現在卻是綠色的。」莎莉說。「妳得施個魔法讓每件東西都回復原狀啊！」

「我需要我的魔法書。」姬達說。她沿著書架一路找下去。她找了找桌子底下，翻了翻坐墊堆。「我把那本魔法書放到那兒去了呢？」

Timothy jumps onto the **windowsill**. He gives a loud meeow.

"Are you trying to tell me something?" asks Gilda. Suddenly she remembers what happened that morning, when she heard someone laughing outside the window. Gilda stares at the blue grass and the **violet** daisies. There are **tiny footprints** on the grass.

"Those look like rabbits' footprints!" she says to herself.

*windowsill*
[ˋwɪndoˌsɪl]
名 窗臺

*violet* [ˋvaɪəlɪt]
形 藍紫色的

*tiny* [ˋtaɪnɪ]
形 細小的

*footprint*
[ˋfutˌprɪnt]
名 足跡

提摩西跳到窗臺上，大聲喵喵叫。
「你是想告訴我什麼事情嗎？」姬達問。
突然間，她想起早晨她聽見窗外有人在笑的事情。她注視著藍色的草地和紫藍色的雛菊。草地上有小小的腳印。
「這看起來像兔子的腳印！」姬達自言自語。

13

"I know what has happened," Gilda tells Sally. "Someone has taken my spell book and I think I know who. Have you seen Bobby and Katie Rabbit this morning?"

"No," says Sally.

"When we find Bobby and Katie, I think we will find the spell book," says Gilda. "Then we can put everything right again. Come and help me look."

「我知道是怎麼回事了。」姬達告訴莎莉。
「有人拿走我的魔法書，我想我知道是誰了。妳今早兒有沒有看見小兔子巴比和凱蒂呢？」

「沒有啊！」莎莉說。

「只要找到巴比和凱蒂，我想我們就能找到那本魔法書了。」姬達說。「那我們就可以把每件東西都恢復原狀了！來幫我找找看吧！」

**G**ilda, Sally and Timothy set out on the **trail** of the **missing** spell book.

Gilda flies along on her broomstick. Sally jumps from tree to tree. Timothy **marches** along with his **whiskers** in the air. They ask everyone they **meet** if they have seen Bobby and Katie.

"No," says Emma **Duckling**.

"No," says Hetty **Hare**.

"No," says Rosie Rabbit.

*trail* [trel]
名 蹤跡

*missing* [`mɪsɪŋ]
形 失蹤的

*march* [mɑrtʃ]
動 大步走

*whisker* [`hwɪskɚ]
名 鬚

*meet* [mit]
動 遇見

*duckling* [`dʌklɪŋ]
名 小鴨子

*hare* [hɛr]
名 野兔

姬達、莎莉和提摩西出發去尋找遺失的魔法書的下落。姬達騎著掃帚沿路飛行；莎莉在樹林間跳來跳去；提摩西則是鬍子翹得高高地大步前進。他們逢人便問有沒有看到巴比和凱蒂。

「沒有耶！」小鴨子艾瑪說。

「沒有啊！」大野兔海蒂說。

「沒有呢！」小兔子羅絲說。

"No," says George Bear who is busy in his garden. "I hope you find your book soon. I cannot **tell** my **plums** from my **peaches** until everything is put right again." Then Timothy begins to sniff at the bushes. He can hear something. He meeows again. Gilda can hear something too. It **sounds** just like two little rabbits crying.

*tell* [tɛl]
動 分辨

*plum* [plʌm]
名 李子

*peach* [pitʃ]
名 桃子

*sound* [saund]
動 聽起來

「沒有喔！」正在花園裡忙著的小熊喬治說。「希望妳很快就能找到妳的書。等一切都正常以後，我才能分辨出李子和桃子。」

這時，提摩西對著灌木叢嗅了起來。他聽見了某種聲音。他又喵喵地叫了起來。姬達也聽見了，聽起來好像是兩隻小兔子在哭泣的聲音。

"Is that you, Katie and Bobby?" calls Gilda.

Katie and Bobby **creep** out from the bushes. Bobby is carrying Gilda's spell book.

"You naughty little rabbits," scolds Gilda. "It was very wrong to take my book without asking."

"We are sorry," sniffs Katie. "We only wanted to **borrow** the book, but we did not want to wake you."

「是你們嗎？凱蒂和巴比？」姬達叫喚著。凱蒂和巴比從樹叢裡躡手躡腳地走了出來，巴比帶著姬達的魔法書。

「你們這些淘氣的小兔子。」姬達罵說。「沒有問一聲就拿走我的書，真是不應該！」

「對不起啦！」凱蒂吸著鼻子說。「我們只是想借這本書，可是又不想把妳吵醒。」

"**W**e wanted to make some magic spells," says Bobby. "We must have **mixed** them **up**, because when we said the magic words the sky turned green. And look!" Katie and Bobby turn around. Their tiny tails are not white, but blue!

"**Never mind**, you can help stir the cauldron while I say the spell that will **change** everything back to **normal** again," says Gilda.

*mix...up*
混淆

*never mind*
不用擔心，沒什麼

*change* [tʃendʒ]
動 改變

*normal* [`nɔrml]
形 正常的

「我們想玩點兒魔法。」巴比說。「我們一定是把它們搞混了，因為我們一唸咒語，天空就變成了綠色的，而且你們看！」凱蒂和巴比轉了個圈，他們的小尾巴不是白色的，竟然是藍色的！

「不要緊！你們幫我攪拌那個大鍋，我邊唸咒語，一切就會恢復正常了。」姬達說。

**E**veryone goes home to Gilda's cottage. They wait while she finds all the magic things she needs.

She needs early morning **dew**, some **moonlight** from a **silver** bottle, some **cobwebs**, and two hairs from a rabbit's tail. "It does not **matter** if they are blue," she says. Then she reads out the magic spell from her book. "**Abracadabra**!" she cries.

*dew* [dju]
名 露水

*moonlight* [ˋmun͵laɪt]
名 月光

*silver* [ˋsɪlvɚ]
形 銀色的

*cobweb* [ˋkɑb͵wɛb]
名 蜘蛛絲

*matter* [ˋmætɚ]
動 重要，有關係

*abracadabra* [͵æbrəkəˋdæbrə] 名
阿布拉卡答布拉（咒語）

大夥兒回到姬達的小木屋。姬達在找齊所有她需要的、具有魔法的東西時，他們就在一旁等著。
她需要的是清晨的露水、一些來自銀瓶子的月光、一些蜘蛛絲，還有兩根兔子尾巴上的毛。
「如果毛是藍色的，也沒關係。」她說。然後她唸出書上的咒語，大叫一聲，「阿布拉卡答布拉！」

They **rush** to the
window. Gilda's spell
has worked! The
sky is blue. The
grass is green.

"Well done," says Sally. "You are a good
witch, Gilda." But Katie and Bobby still have
their blue tails.
"They will be white again in a few days," Gilda
says to them. "That will teach you not to
**meddle** with magic!"

*rush* [rʌʃ]
動 衝

*meddle* [ˋmɛdl̩]
動 亂動

大夥兒衝到窗邊。姬達的咒語靈驗了！天
空是藍色的，草地是綠色的！
「做得好吧！」莎莉說。「妳真是個好棒的
巫婆啊！姬達。」可是凱蒂和巴比的尾巴
仍然是藍色的。
「它們過幾天就會變回白色了。」姬達對
他們說。「這樣才可以教訓你們，不可以
亂動魔法啊！」

# Say these words again.

| | |
|---|---|
| forest | right |
| snooze | cushions |
| magic | laughing |
| cottage | whiskers |
| window | suddenly |
| distance | borrow |
| sweeten | meddle |

# What can you see?

**broomstick**

**cauldron**

**spell book**

**cat**

**crystal ball**

# 只要你選對了英文辭典
# 學英文不難

## 三民皇冠英漢辭典 （革新版）

—— 大學教授一致推薦，最適合中學生的辭典！

- 明顯標示中學生必學的507個單字和最常犯的錯誤，淺顯又易懂！
- 收錄豐富詞條及例句，幫助你輕鬆閱讀課外讀物！
- 詳盡的「參考」及「印象」欄，讓你體會英語的「弦外之音」！

## 三民精解英漢辭典

—— 一本真正賞心悅目，趣味橫生的英漢辭典！

- 常用基本字彙以較大字體標示，並搭配豐富的使用範例。
- 以五大句型為基礎，讓你更容易活用動詞型態。
- 豐富的漫畫式插圖，讓你輕鬆快樂地學習。

網際網路位址　http :∕∕ www. sanmin. com. tw

© 巫婆姬達

著作人　Terry Dinning
繪圖者　Angela Kincaid
譯　者　陳培真
發行人　劉振強
著作財　三民書局股份有限公司
產權人
　　　　臺北市復興北路三八六號
發行所　三民書局股份有限公司
　　　　地址／臺北市復興北路三八六號
　　　　電話／二五〇〇六六〇〇
　　　　郵撥／〇〇〇九九九八——五號
印刷所　三民書局股份有限公司
門市部　復北店／臺北市復興北路三八六號
　　　　重南店／臺北市重慶南路一段六十一號
初　版　中華民國八十八年十一月
編　號　S85540
定　價　新臺幣壹佰陸拾元整
行政院新聞局登記證局版臺業字第〇二〇〇號

有著作權．不准侵害

ISBN　957-14-3085-4 （精裝）